To Whom This

1898

Edward Bellamy

Alpha Editions

This edition published in 2024

ISBN : 9789357963770

Design and Setting By
Alpha Editions
www.alphaedis.com
Email - info@alphaedis.com

Contents

TO WHOM THIS MAY COME

BY EDWARD BELLAMY

1898

It is now about a year since I took passage at Calcutta in the ship Adelaide for New York. We had baffling weather till New Amsterdam Island was sighted, where we took a new point of departure. Three days later, a terrible gale struck us Four days we flew before it, whither, no one knew, for neither sun, moon, nor stars were at any time visible, and we could take no observation. Toward midnight of the fourth day, the glare of lightning revealed the Adelaide in a hopeless position, close in upon a low-lying shore, and driving straight toward it. All around and astern far out to sea was such a maze of rocks and shoals that it was a miracle we had come so far. Presently the ship struck, and almost instantly went to pieces, so great was the violence of the sea. I gave myself up for lost, and was indeed already past the worst of drowning, when I was recalled to consciousness by being thrown with a tremendous shock upon the beach. I had just strength enough to drag myself above the reach of the waves, and then I fell down and knew no more.

When I awoke, the storm was over. The sun, already halfway up the sky, had dried my clothing, and renewed the vigor of my bruised and aching limbs. On sea or shore I saw no vestige of my ship or my companions, of whom I appeared the sole survivor. I was not, however, alone. A group of persons, apparently the inhabitants of the country, stood near, observing me with looks of friendliness which at once freed me from apprehension as to my treatment at their hands. They were a white and handsome people, evidently of a high order of civilization, though I recognized in them the traits of no race with which I was familiar.

Seeing that it was evidently their idea of etiquette to leave it to strangers to open conversation, I addressed them in English, but failed to elicit any response beyond deprecating smiles. I then accosted them successively in the French, German, Italian, Spanish, Dutch, and Portuguese tongues, but with no better results. I began to be very much puzzled as to what could possibly be the nationality of a white and evidently civilized race to which no one of the tongues of the great seafaring nations was intelligible. The oddest thing of all was the unbroken silence with which they contemplated my efforts to open communication with them. It was as if they were agreed not to give me a clue to their language by even a whisper; for while they regarded one another with looks of smiling intelligence, they did not once open their lips. But if this behavior suggested that they were amusing themselves at my expense, that presumption was negatived by the unmistakable friendliness and sympathy which their whole bearing expressed.

A most extraordinary conjecture occurred to me. Could it be that these strange people were dumb? Such a freak of nature as an entire race thus afflicted had never indeed been heard of, but who could say what wonders the unexplored vasts of the great Southern Ocean might thus far have hid from human ken? Now, among the scraps of useless information which lumbered my mind was an acquaintance with the deaf-and-dumb alphabet, and forthwith I began to spell out with my fingers some of the phrases I had already uttered to so little effect. My resort to the sign language overcame the last remnant of gravity in the already profusely smiling group. The small boys now rolled on the ground in convulsions of mirth, while the grave and reverend seniors, who had hitherto kept them in check, were fain momentarily to avert their faces, and I could see their bodies shaking with laughter. The greatest clown in the world never received a more flattering tribute to his powers to amuse than had been called forth by mine to make myself understood. Naturally, however, I was not flattered, but on the contrary entirely discomfited. Angry I could not well be, for the deprecating manner in which all, excepting of course the boys, yielded to their perception of the ridiculous, and the distress they showed at their failure in self-control, made me seem the aggressor. It was as if they were very sorry for me, and ready to put themselves wholly at my service, if I would only refrain from reducing them to a state of disability by being so exquisitely absurd. Certainly this evidently amiable race had a very embarrassing way of receiving strangers.

Just at this moment, when my bewilderment was fast verging on exasperation, relief came. The circle opened, and a little elderly man, who had evidently come in haste, confronted me, and, bowing very politely, addressed me in English. His voice was the most pitiable abortion of a voice I had ever heard. While having all the defects in articulation of a child's who is just beginning to talk, it was not even a child's in strength of tone, being in fact a mere alternation of squeaks and whispers inaudible a rod away. With some difficulty I was, however, able to follow him pretty nearly.

"As the official interpreter," he said, "I extend you a cordial welcome to these islands. I was sent for as soon as you were discovered, but being at some distance, I was unable to arrive until this moment. I regret this, as my presence would have saved you embarrassment. My countrymen desire me to intercede with you to pardon the wholly involuntary and uncontrollable mirth provoked by your attempts to communicate with them. You see, they understood you perfectly well, but could not answer you."

"Merciful heavens!" I exclaimed, horrified to find my surmise correct; "can it be that they are all thus afflicted? Is it possible that you are the only man among them who has the power of speech?"

Again it appeared that, quite unintentionally, I had said something excruciatingly funny; for at my speech there arose a sound of gentle laughter from the group, now augmented to quite an assemblage, which drowned the plashing of the waves on the beach at our feet. Even the interpreter smiled.

"Do they think it so amusing to be dumb?" I asked.

"They find it very amusing," replied the interpreter, "that their inability to speak should be regarded by any one as an affliction; for it is by the voluntary disuse of the organs of articulation that they have lost the power of speech, and, as a consequence, the ability even to understand speech."

"But," said I, somewhat puzzled by this statement, "did n't you just tell me that they understood me, though they could not reply, and are they not laughing now at what I just said?"

"It is you they understood, not your words," answered the interpreter. "Our speech now is gibberish to them, as unintelligible in itself as the growling of animals; but they know what we are saying, because they know our thoughts. You must know that these are the islands of the mind-readers."

Such were the circumstances of my introduction to this extraordinary people. The official interpreter being charged by virtue of his office with the first entertainment of shipwrecked members of the talking nations, I became his guest, and passed a number of days under his roof before going out to any considerable extent among the people. My first impression had been the somewhat oppressive one that the power to read the thoughts of others could be possessed only by beings of a superior order to man. It was the first effort of the interpreter to disabuse me of this notion. It appeared from his account that the experience of the mind-readers was a case simply of a slight acceleration, from special causes, of the course of universal human evolution, which in time was destined to lead to the disuse of speech and the substitution of direct mental vision on the part of all races. This rapid evolution of these islanders was accounted for by their peculiar origin and circumstances.

Some three centuries before Christ, one of the Parthian kings of Persia, of the dynasty of the Arsacid, undertook a persecution of the soothsayers and magicians in his realms. These people were credited with supernatural powers by popular prejudice, but in fact were merely persons of special gifts in the way of hypnotizing, mind-reading, thought transference, and such arts, which they exercised for their own gain.

Too much in awe of the soothsayers to do them outright violence, the king resolved to banish them, and to this end put them, with their families, on ships and sent them to Ceylon. When, however, the fleet was in the neighborhood of that island, a great storm scattered it, and one of the ships, after being driven for many days before the tempest, was wrecked upon one of an archipelago of uninhabited islands far to the south, where the survivors settled. Naturally, the posterity of the parents possessed of such peculiar gifts had developed extraordinary psychical powers.

Having set before them the end of evolving a new and advanced order of humanity, they had aided the development of these powers by a rigid system of stirpiculture. The result was that, after a few centuries, mind-reading became so general that language fell into disuse as a means of communicating ideas. For many generations the power of speech still remained voluntary, but gradually the vocal organs had become atrophied, and for several hundred years the power of articulation had been wholly lost. Infants for a few months after birth did, indeed, still emit inarticulate cries, but at an age when in less advanced races these cries began to be articulate, the children of the mind-readers developed the power of direct vision, and ceased to attempt to use the voice.

The fact that the existence of the mind-readers had never been found out by the rest of the world was explained by two considerations. In the first place, the group of islands was small, and occupied a corner of the Indian Ocean quite out of the ordinary track of ships. In the second place, the approach to the islands was rendered so desperately perilous by terrible currents, and the maze of outlying rocks and shoals, that it was next to impossible for any ship to touch their shores save as a wreck. No ship at least had ever done so in the two thousand years since the mind-readers' own arrival, and the Adelaide had made the one hundred and twenty-third such wreck.

Apart from motives of humanity, the mind-readers made strenuous efforts to rescue shipwrecked persons, for from them alone, through the interpreters, could they obtain information of the outside world. Little enough this proved when, as often happened, the sole survivor of the shipwreck was some ignorant sailor, who had no news to communicate beyond the latest varieties of forecastle blasphemy. My hosts gratefully assured me that, as a person of some little education, they considered me a veritable godsend. No less a task was mine than to relate to them the history of the world for the past two centuries, and often did I wish, for their sakes, that I had made a more exact study of it.

It is solely for the purpose of communicating with shipwrecked strangers of the talking nations that the office of the interpreters exists. When, as from time to time happens, a child is born with some powers of articulation, he is set apart, and trained to talk in the interpreters' college. Of course the partial atrophy of the vocal organs, from which even the best interpreters suffer, renders many of the sounds of language impossible for them. None, for instance, can pronounce *v*, *f*, or *s*; and as to the sound represented by *th*, it is five generations since the last interpreter lived who could utter it. But for the occasional inter-marriage of shipwrecked strangers with the island-ers, it is probable that the supply of interpreters would have long ere this quite failed.

I imagine that the very unpleasant sensations which followed the realization that I was among people who, while inscrutable to me, knew my every thought, were very much what any one would have experienced in the same case. They were very comparable to the panic which accidental nudity causes a person among races whose custom it is to conceal the figure with drapery. I wanted to run away and hide myself. If I analyzed my feeling, it did not seem to arise so much from the consciousness of any particularly heinous secrets, as from the knowledge of a swarm of fatuous, ill-natured, and unseemly thoughts and half thoughts concerning those around me, and concerning myself, which it was insufferable that any person should peruse in however benevolent a spirit. But while my chagrin and distress on this account were at first intense, they were also very shortlived, for almost immediately I discovered that the very knowledge that my mind was overlooked by others operated to check thoughts that might be painful to them, and that, too, without more effort of the will than a kindly person exerts to check the utterance of disagreeable remarks. As a very few lessons in the elements of courtesy cures a decent person of inconsiderate speaking, so a brief experience among the mind-readers went far in my case to check inconsiderate thinking. It must not be supposed, however, that courtesy among the mind-readers prevents them from thinking pointedly and freely concerning one another upon serious occasions, any more than the finest courtesy among the talking races restrains them from speaking to one another with entire plainness when it it desirable to do so. Indeed, among the mind-readers, politeness never can extend to the point of insincerity, as among talking nations, seeing that it is always one another's real and inmost thought that they read. I may fitly mention here, though it was not till later that I fully understood why it must necessarily be so, that one need feel far less chagrin at the complete revelation of his weaknesses to a mind-reader than at the slightest betrayal of them to one of another race. For the very reason that the mind-reader reads all your thoughts, particular thoughts are judged with reference to the general tenor of thought. Your characteristic and habitual frame of mind is what he takes account of. No one need fear being misjudged by a mind-reader on account of sentiments or emotions which are not representative of the real character or general attitude. Justice may, indeed, be said to be a necessary consequence of mind-reading.

As regards the interpreter himself, the instinct of courtesy was not long needed to check wanton or offensive thoughts. In all my life before, I had been very slow to form friendships, but before I had been three days in the company of this stranger of a strange race, I had become enthusiastically devoted to him. It was impossible not to be. The peculiar joy of friendship is the sense of being understood by our friend as we are not by others, and yet of being loved in spite of the understanding. Now here was one whose every word testified to a knowledge of my secret thoughts and motives which the oldest and nearest of my former friends had never, and could never, have approximated. Had such a knowledge bred in him contempt of me, I should neither have blamed him nor been at all surprised. Judge, then, whether the cordial friendliness which he showed was likely to leave me indifferent.

Imagine my incredulity when he informed me that our friendship was not based upon more than ordinary mutual suitability of temperaments. The faculty of mind-reading, he explained, brought minds so close together, and so heightened sympathy, that the lowest order of friendship between mind-readers implied a mutual delight such as only rare friends enjoyed among other races. He assured me that later on, when I came to know others of his race, I should find, by the far greater intensity of sympathy and affection I should conceive for some of them, how true this saying was.

It may be inquired how, on beginning to mingle with the mind-readers in general, I managed to communicate with them, seeing that, while they could read my thoughts, they could not, like the interpreter, respond to them by speech. I must here explain that, while these people have no use for a spoken language, a written language is needful for purposes of record. They consequently all know how to write. Do they, then, write Persian? Luckily for me, no. It appears that, for a long period after mind-reading was fully developed, not only was spoken language disused, but also written, no records whatever having been kept during this period. The delight of the people in the newly found power of direct mind-to-mind vision, whereby pictures of the total mental state were communicated, instead of the imperfect descriptions of single thoughts which words at best could give, induced an invincible distaste for the laborious impotence of language.

When, however, the first intellectual intoxication had, after several generations, somewhat sobered down, it was recognized that records of the past were desirable, and that the despised medium of words was needful to preserve it. Persian had meanwhile been wholly forgotten. In order to avoid the prodigious task of inventing a complete new language, the institution of the interpreters was now set up, with the idea of acquiring through them a knowledge of some of the languages of the outside world from the mariners wrecked on the islands.

Owing to the fact that most of the castaway ships were English, a better knowledge of that tongue was acquired than of any other, and it was adopted as the written language of the people. As a rule, my acquaintances wrote slowly and laboriously, and yet the fact that they knew exactly what was in my mind rendered their responses so apt that, in my conversations with the slowest speller of them all, the interchange of thought was as rapid and incomparably more accurate and satisfactory than the fastest talkers attain to.

It was but a very short time after I had begun to extend my acquaintance among the mind-readers before I discovered how truly the interpreter had told me that I should find others to whom, on account of greater natural congeniality, I should become more strongly attached than I had been to him. This was in no wise, however, because I loved him less, but them more. I would fain write particularly of some of these beloved friends, comrades of my heart, from whom I first learned the undreamed-of possibilities of human friendship, and how ravishing the satisfactions of sympathy may be. Who, among those who may read this, has not known that sense of a gulf fixed between soul and soul which mocks love I Who has not felt that loneliness which oppresses the heart that loves it best! Think no longer that this gulf is eternally fixed, or is any necessity of human nature. It has no existence for the race of our fellow-men which I describe, and by that fact we may be assured that eventually it will be bridged also for us. Like the touch of shoulder to shoulder, like the clasping of hands, is the contact of their minds and their sensation of sympathy.

I say that I would fain speak more particularly of some of my friends, but waning strength forbids, and moreover, now that I think of it, another consideration would render any comparison of their characters rather confusing than instructive to a reader. This is the fact that, in common with the rest of the mind-readers, they had no names. Every one had, indeed, an arbitrary sign for his designation in records, but it has no sound value. A register of these names is kept, so they can at any time be ascertained, but it is very common to meet persons who have forgotten titles which are used solely for biographical and official purposes. For social intercourse names are of course superfluous, for these people accost one another merely by a mental act of attention, and refer to third persons by transferring their mental pictures,— something as dumb persons might by means of photographs. Something so, I say, for in the pictures of one another's personalities which the mind-readers conceive, the physical aspect, as might be expected with people who directly contemplate each other's minds and hearts, is a subordinate element.

I have already told how my first qualms of morbid self-consciousness at knowing that my mind was an open book to all around me disappeared as I learned that the very completeness of the disclosure of my thoughts and motives was a guarantee that I would be judged with a fairness and a sympathy such as even self-judgment cannot pretend to, affected as that is by so many subtle reactions. The assurance of being so judged by every one might well seem an inestimable privilege to one accustomed to a world in which not even the tenderest love is any pledge of comprehension, and yet I soon discovered that open-mindedness had a still greater profit than this. How shall I describe the delightful exhilaration of moral health and cleanness, the breezy oxygenated mental condition, which resulted from the consciousness that I had absolutely nothing concealed! Truly I may say that I enjoyed myself. I think surely that no one needs to have had my marvelous experience to sympathize with this portion of it. Are we not all ready to agree that this having a curtained chamber where we may go to grovel, out of the sight of our fellows, troubled only by a vague apprehension that God may look over the top, is the most demoralizing incident in the human condition? It is the existence within the soul of this secure refuge of lies which has always been the despair of the saint and the exultation of the knave. It is the foul cellar which taints the whole house above, be it never so fine.

What stronger testimony could there be to the instinctive consciousness that concealment is debauching, and openness our only cure, than the world-old conviction of the virtue of confession for the soul, and that the uttermost exposing of one's worst and foulest is the first step toward moral health? The wickedest man, if he could but somehow attain to writhe himself inside out as to his soul, so that its full sickness could be seen, would feel ready for a new life. Nevertheless, owing to the utter impotence of the words to convey mental conditions in their totality, or to give other than mere distortions of them, confession is, we must needs admit, but a mockery of that longing for self-revelation to which it testifies. But think what health and soundness there must be for souls among a people who see in every face a conscience which, unlike their own, they cannot sophisticate, who confess one another with a glance, and shrive with a smile! Ah, friends, let me now predict, though ages may elapse before the slow event shall justify me, that in no way will the mutual vision of minds, when at last it shall be perfected, so enhance the blessedness of mankind as by rending the veil of self, and leaving no spot of darkness in the mind for lies to hide in. Then shall the soul no longer be a coal smoking among ashes, but a star in a crystal sphere.

From what I have said of the delights which friendship among the mind-readers derives from the perfection of the mental rapport, it may be imagined how intoxicating must be the experience when one of the friends is a woman, and the subtle attractions and correspondences of sex touch with passion the intellectual sympathy. With my first venturing into society I had begun, to their extreme amusement, to fall in love with the women right and left. In the perfect frankness which is the condition of all intercourse among this people, these adorable women told me that what I felt was only friendship, which was a very good thing, but wholly different from love, as I should well know if I were beloved. It was difficult to believe that the melting emotions which I had experienced in their company were the result merely of the friendly and kindly attitude of their minds toward mine; but when I found that I was affected in the same way by every gracious woman I met, I had to make up my mind that they must be right about it, and that I should have to adapt myself to a world in which, friendship being a passion, love must needs be nothing less than rapture.

The homely proverb, "Every Jack has his Gill," may, I suppose, be taken to mean that for all men there are certain women expressly suited by mental and moral as well as by physical constitution. It is a thought painful, rather than cheering, that this may be the truth, so altogether do the chances preponderate against the ability of these elect ones to recognize each other even if they meet, seeing that speech is so inadequate and so misleading a medium of self-revelation. But among the mind-readers, the search for one's ideal mate is a quest reasonably sure of being crowned with success, and no one dreams of wedding unless it be; for so to do, they consider, would be to throw away the choicest blessing of life, and not alone to wrong themselves and their unfound mates, but likewise those whom they themselves and those undiscovered mates might wed. Therefore, passionate pilgrims, they go from isle to isle till they find each other, and, as the population of the islands is but small, the pilgrimage is not often long.

When I met her first we were in company, and I was struck by the sudden stir and the looks and smiling interest with which all around turned and regarded us, the women with moistened eyes. They had read her thought when she saw me, but this I did not know, neither what was the custom in these matters, till afterward. But I knew, from the moment she first fixed her eyes on me, and I felt her mind brooding upon mine, how truly I had been told by those other women that the feeling with which they had inspired me was not love.

With people who become acquainted at a glance, and old friends in an hour, wooing is naturally not a long process. Indeed, it may be said that between lovers among mind-readers there is no wooing, but merely recognition. The day after we met, she became mine.

Perhaps I cannot better illustrate how subordinate the merely physical element is in the impression which mind-readers form of their friends than by mentioning an incident that occurred some months after our union. This was my discovery, wholly by accident, that my love, in whose society I had almost constantly been, had not the least idea what was the color of my eyes, or whether my hair and complexion were light or dark. Of course, as soon as I asked her the question, she read the answer in my mind, but she admitted that she had previously had no distinct impression on those points. On the other hand, if in the blackest midnight I should come to her, she would not need to ask who the comer was. It is by the mind, not the eye, that these people know one another. It is really only in their relations to soulless and inanimate things that they need eyes at all.

It must not be supposed that their disregard of one another's bodily aspect grows out of any ascetic sentiment. It is merely a necessary consequence of their power of directly apprehending mind, that whenever mind is closely associated with matter the latter is comparatively neglected on account of the greater interest of the former, suffering as lesser things always do when placed in immediate contrast with greater. Art is with them confined to the inanimate, the human form having, for the reason mentioned, ceased to inspire the artist. It will be naturally and quite correctly inferred that among such a race physical beauty is not the important factor in human fortune and felicity that it elsewhere is. The absolute openness of their minds and hearts to one another makes their happiness far more dependent on the moral and mental qualities of their companions than upon their physical. A genial temperament, a wide-grasping, godlike intellect, a poet soul, are incomparably more fascinating to them than the most dazzling combination conceivable of mere bodily graces.

A woman of mind and heart has no more need of beauty to win love in these islands than a beauty elsewhere of mind or heart. I should mention here, perhaps, that this race, which makes so little account of physical beauty, is itself a singularly handsome one. This is owing doubtless in part to the absolute compatibility of temperaments in all the marriages, and partly also to the reaction upon the body of a state of ideal mental and moral health and placidity.

Not being myself a mind-reader, the fact that my love was rarely beautiful in form and face had doubtless no little part in attracting my devotion. This, of course, she knew, as she knew all my thoughts, and, knowing my limitations, tolerated and forgave the element of sensuousness in my passion. But if it must have seemed to her so little worthy in comparison with the high spiritual communion which her race know as love, to me it became, by virtue of her almost superhuman relation to me, an ecstasy more ravishing surely than any lover of my race tasted before. The ache at the heart of the intensest love is the impotence of words to make it perfectly understood to its object. But my passion was without this pang, for my heart was absolutely open to her I loved. Lovers may imagine, but I cannot describe, the ecstatic thrill of communion into which this consciousness transformed every tender emotion. As I considered what mutual love must be where both parties are mind-readers, I realized the high communion which my sweet companion had sacrificed for me.

She might indeed comprehend her lover and his love for her, but the higher satisfaction of knowing that she was comprehended by him and her love understood, she had foregone. For that I should ever attain the power of mind-reading was out of the question, the faculty never having been developed in a single lifetime.

Why my inability should move my dear companion to such depths of pity I was not able fully to understand until I learned that mind-reading is chiefly held desirable, not for the knowledge of others which it gives its possessors, but for the self-knowledge which is its reflex effect. Of all they see in the minds of others, that which concerns them most is the reflection of themselves, the photographs of their own characters. The most obvious consequence of the self-knowledge thus forced upon them is to render them alike incapable of self-conceit or self-depreciation. Every one must needs always think of himself as he is, being no more able to do otherwise than is a man in a hall of mirrors to cherish delusions as to his personal appearance.

But self-knowledge means to the mind-readers much more than this,— nothing less, indeed, than a shifting of the sense of identity. When a man sees himself in a mirror, he is compelled to distinguish between the bodily self he sees and his real self, which is within and unseen. When in turn the mind-reader comes to see the mental and moral self reflected in other minds as in mirrors, the same thing happens. He is compelled to distinguish between this mental and moral self which has been made objective to him, and can be contemplated by him as impartially as if it were another's, from the inner ego which still remains subjective, unseen, and indefinable. In this inner ego the mind-readers recognize the essential identity and being, the noumenal self, the core of the soul, and the true hiding of its eternal life, to which the mind as well as the body is but the garment of a day.

The effect of such a philosophy as this—which, indeed, with the mind-readers is rather an instinctive consciousness than a philosophy —must obviously be to impart a sense of wonderful superiority to the vicissitudes of this earthly state, and a singular serenity in the midst of the haps and mishaps which threaten or befall the personality. They did indeed appear to me, as I never dreamed men could attain to be, lords of themselves.

It was because I might not hope to attain this enfranchisement from the false ego of the apparent self, without which life seemed to her race scarcely worth living, that my love so pitied me.

But I must hasten on, leaving a thousand things unsaid, to relate the lamentable catastrophe to which it is owing that, instead of being still a resident of those blessed islands, in the full enjoyment of that intimate and ravishing companionship which by contrast would forever dim the pleasures of all other human society, I recall the bright picture as a memory under other skies.

Among a people who are compelled by the very constitution of their minds to put themselves in the places of others, the sympathy which is the inevitable consequence of perfect comprehension renders envy, hatred, and uncharitableness impossible. But of course there are people less genially constituted than others, and these are necessarily the objects of a certain distaste on the part of associates. Now, owing to the unhindered impact of minds upon one another, the anguish of persons so regarded, despite the tenderest consideration of those about them, is so great that they beg the grace of exile, that, being out of the way, people may think less frequently upon them. There are numerous small islets, scarcely more than rocks, lying to the north of the archipelago, and on these the unfortunates are permitted to live. Only one lives on each islet, as they cannot endure each other even as well as the more happily constituted can endure them. From time to time supplies of food are taken to them, and of course, any time they wish to take the risk, they are permitted to return to society.

Now, as I have said, the fact which, even more than their out-of-the-way location, makes the islands of the mind-readers unapproachable, is the violence with which the great antarctic current, owing probably to some configuration of the ocean bed, together with the innumerable rocks and shoals, flows through and about the archipelago.

Ships making the islands from the southward are caught by this current and drawn among the rocks, to their almost certain destruction; while, owing to the violence with which the current sets to the north, it is not possible to approach at all from that direction, or at least it has never been accomplished. Indeed, so powerful are the currents that even the boats which cross the narrow straits between the main islands and the islets of the unfortunate, to carry the latter their supplies, are ferried over by cables, not trusting to oar or sail.

The brother of my love had charge of one of the boats engaged in this transportation, and, being desirous of visiting the islets, I accepted an invitation to accompany him on one of his trips. I know nothing of how the accident happened, but in the fiercest part of the current of one of the straits we parted from the cable and were swept out to sea. There was no question of stemming the boiling current, our utmost endeavors barely sufficing to avoid being dashed to pieces on the rocks. From the first, there was no hope of our winning back to the land, and so swiftly did we drift that by noon— the accident having befallen in the morning—the islands, which are low-lying, had sunk beneath the southwestern horizon.

Among these mind-readers, distance is not an insuperable obstacle to the transfer of thought. My companion was in communication with our friends, and from time to time conveyed to me messages of anguish from my dear love; for, being well aware of the nature of the currents and the unapproachableness of the islands, those we had left behind, as well as we ourselves, knew well we should see each other's faces no more. For five days we continued to drift to the northwest, in no danger of starvation, owing to our lading of provisions, but constrained to unintermitting watch and ward by the roughness of the weather. On the fifth day my companion died from exposure and exhaustion. He died very quietly,—indeed, with great appearance of relief. The life of the mind-readers while yet they are in the body is so largely spiritual that the idea of an existence wholly so, which seems vague and chill to us, suggests to them a state only slightly more refined than they already know on earth.

After that I suppose I must have fallen into an unconscious state, from which I roused to find myself on an American ship bound for New York, surrounded by people whose only means of communicating with one another is to keep up while together a constant clatter of hissing, guttural, and explosive noises, eked out by all manner of facial contortions and bodily gestures. I frequently find myself staring open-mouthed at those who address me, too much struck by their grotesque appearance to bethink myself of replying.

I find that I shall not live out the voyage, and I do not care to. From my experience of the people on the ship, I can judge how I should fare on land amid the stunning Babel of a nation of talkers. And my friends, —God bless them! how lonely I should feel in their very presence! Nay, what satisfaction or consolation, what but bitter mockery, could I ever more find in such human sympathy and companionship as suffice others and once sufficed me,—I who have seen and known what I have seen and known! Ah, yes, doubtless it is far better I should die; but the knowledge of the things that I have seen I feel should not perish with me. For hope's sake, men should not miss the glimpse of the higher, sun-bathed reaches of the upward path they plod. So thinking, I have written out some account of my wonderful experience, though briefer far, by reason of my weakness, than fits the greatness of the matter. The captain seems an honest, well-meaning man, and to him I shall confide the narrative, charging him, on touching shore, to see it safely in the hands of some one who will bring it to the world's ear.

Note.—The extent of my own connection with the foregoing document is sufficiently indicated by the author himself in the final paragraph.— E.B.

———————————

Milton Keynes UK
Ingram Content Group UK Ltd.
UKHW010759110624
444053UK00004B/343